This
Harry
book belongs to

BENJAMIN. HARRIS
....
I AM 4

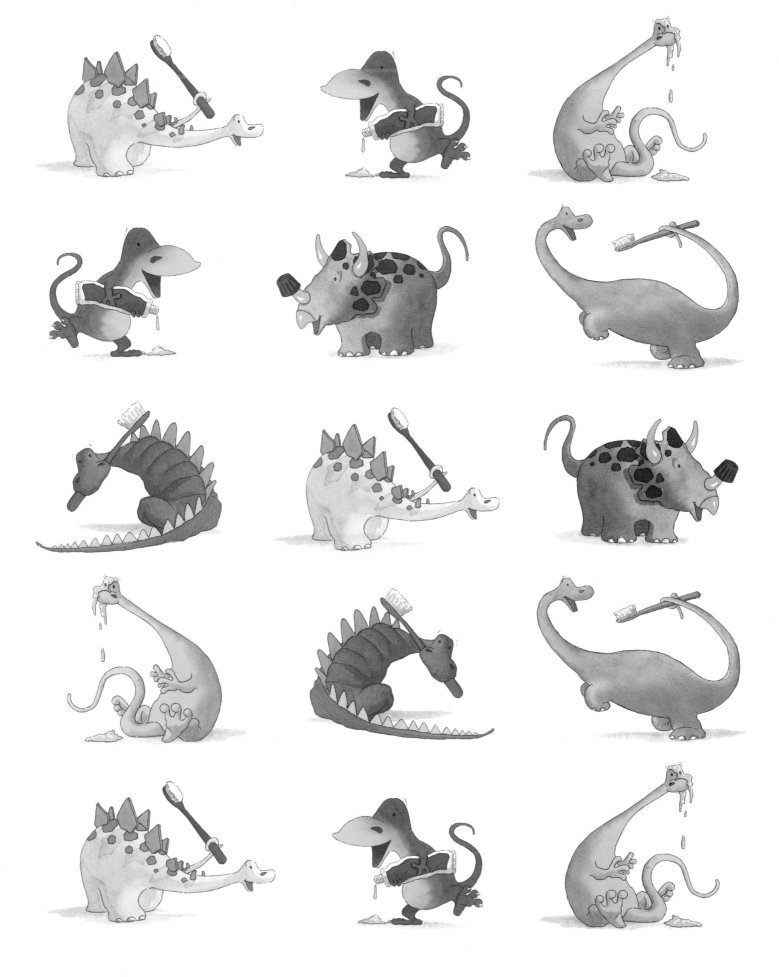

For Jack Drake,
my favourite dentist
I.W.

For Mr Jon Harris
who is a good brusher
A.R.

PUFFIN BOOKS

Published by the Penguin Group
Penguin Books Ltd, 80 Strand, London WC2R 0RL, England
Penguin Group (USA), Inc., 375 Hudson Street, New York, New York 10014, USA
Penguin Books Australia Ltd, 250 Camberwell Road, Camberwell, Victoria 3124, Australia
Penguin Books Canada Ltd, 10 Alcorn Avenue, Toronto, Ontario, Canada M4V 3B2
Penguin Books India (P) Ltd, 11 Community Centre, Panchsheel Park, New Delhi – 110 017, India
Penguin Books (NZ) Ltd, Cnr Rosedale and Airborne Roads, Albany, Auckland, New Zealand
Penguin Books (South Africa) (Pty) Ltd, 24 Sturdee Avenue, Rosebank 2196, South Africa

Penguin Books Ltd, Registered Offices: 80 Strand, London WC2R 0RL, England

www.penguin.com

First published in hardback by Gullane Children's Books 2001
First published in paperback by Gullane Children's Books 2002
First published in Puffin Books 2003
5 7 9 10 8 6 4

Text copyright © Ian Whybrow, 2001
Illustrations copyright © Adrian Reynolds, 2001
All rights reserved

The moral right of the author and illustrator has been asserted

Manufactured in China

British Library Cataloguing in Publication Data
A CIP catalogue record for this book is available from the British Library

ISBN 0–140–56981–2

Harry and the Dinosaurs Say "Raahh!"

Ian Whybrow and Adrian Reynolds

PUFFIN

Mum had her coat on,
but Harry was being slow.
They were going to see
Mr Drake, the dentist.

Harry was only a bit scared.
That was because of Sam
showing him her filling.

Harry wanted to take his dinosaurs,
but they were hiding all over the place.
He called all their names.

He said, "Get in the bucket, my Stegosaurus."
And out came Stegosaurus from under
the pillow.

He said, "Get in the bucket, my Triceratops."
And out came Triceratops from inside
the drawer.

And one by one, Apatosaurus and Scelidosaurus
and Anchisaurus all came out of their hiding
places and they jumped into the bucket.

All except for Tyrannosaurus. He didn't want
to go because he had a lot of teeth.
He thought Mr Drake might do drilling on them.

Harry said, "Don't worry, because when we get there,
I shall press a magic button on my bucket,
and that will make you grow big."

In the waiting room, the nurse said,
"Hello, Harry. Are you a good boy?"
Harry said, "I am, but my dinosaurs bite."

Then Mr Drake called,
"Next please!"

The nurse took Harry into Mr Drake's room.
Harry wasn't sure about the big chair. He thought
maybe that was where Mr Drake did the drilling.
  "Come and have a ride in my chair," said Mr Drake.
"It goes up and down."
  Harry didn't want to ride.
  "Would one of your dinosaurs like a go?"
asked Mr Drake.

Harry put Tyrannosaurus on the chair.
He whispered to him not to worry,
then he pressed the magic button . . .
Tyrannosaurus grew VERY BIG!

"Open wide," said Mr Drake,
and then he turned around . . .

"RAAAAHH!" said Tyrannosaurus.
"Help!" cried Mr Drake, hiding behind
the door. "Harry, what shall I do?"

Harry pressed the magic button.
Straight away, Tyrannosaurus
went back to being bucket-sized.

Harry felt safer now about getting
into the chair, so he climbed in with
his bucket. Then Harry and his dinosaurs
all had a ride together.
They opened their mouths wide for
Mr Drake and all went, 'RAAAAHH!'
Mr Drake said, "What a lot of teeth!
Will they bite me?"
Harry said, "They only bite drills."

"You are all good brushers," said Mr Drake,
"so no drills today, only a look
and a rinse."

All the dinosaurs liked riding and they liked rinsing.
    "Another bucket of mouthwash, Joan!"
called Mr Drake.

Going home, Mum let Harry choose a book
from the library for being so good.
    "Let's have a shark book!" said Harry.
    "RAAAAHH!" said the dinosaurs.
"Sharp teeth! We like sharks!"

ENDOSAURUS

Look out for all of Harry's adventures!

ISBN 0140569804

Harry and the Bucketful of Dinosaurs
Harry finds some old, plastic dinosaurs and cleans them, finds out their names and takes them everywhere with him – until, one day, they get lost... Will he ever find them?

Harry and the Snow King
There's just enough snow for Harry to build a very small snow king. But then the snow king disappears – who's kidnapped him?

ISBN 0140569863

ISBN 0140569820

Harry and the Robots
Harry's robot is sent to the toy hospital to be fixed, so Harry and Nan decide to make a new one. When Nan has to go to hospital, Harry knows just how to help her get better!

Harry and the Dinosaurs say "Raahh!"
Harry's dinosaurs are acting strangely. They're hiding all over the house, refusing to come out... Could it be because today is the day of Harry's dentist appointment?

ISBN 0140569812

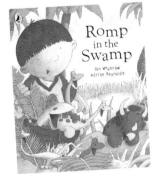

ISBN 0140569847

Harry and the Dinosaurs Romp in the Swamp
Harry has to play at Charlie's house and doesn't want to share his dinosaurs. But when Charlie builds a fantastic swamp, Harry and the dinosaurs can't help but join in the fun!

Harry and the Dinosaurs make a Christmas Wish
Harry and the dinosaurs would *love* to own a duckling. They wait till Christmas and make a special wish, but Santa leaves them something even more exciting...!

ISBN 0141380179 (hbk)
ISBN 0140569529 (pbk)

ISBN 0140569839

ISBN 0140569855

Harry and the Dinosaurs play Hide-and-Seek
Harry and the Dinosaurs have a Very Busy Day
Join in with Harry and his dinosaurs for some peep-through fold-out fun! These exciting books about shapes and colours make learning easy!